Then We'd Be Happy

A NOVEL

Al Riske

This is a work of fiction. Names, characters, places, and incidents are either the product of the author's imagination or are used fictitiously. Any resemblance to actual persons, living or dead, business establishments, events, or locales is entirely coincidental.

Copyright 2017 by Al Riske

All rights reserved

Cover design and photography by Joanne Riske

ISBN: 9781096001249

Then We'd Be Happy

MAD ENOUGH

We're in this Denny's on El Camino somewhere. We're ravenous and loud. Wired but also tired.

Spencer says: "Women need to understand the difference between being friendly and flirting, because most men take it as being into them, and then they want to punch a baby."

The hostess who seats us gives him a sad-eyed look as she passes out the menus.

Marty says: "Fuck, yeah, brother!"

"Had to be said."

We watch the hostess walk away. She's older but kind of hot.

"Already have a boyfriend? Let me know that up front, before I get my hopes up," Spencer says to no one in particular—to womankind at large.

Nita, who hangs with us sometimes, gives Spencer the same sad-eyed look the hostess did.

"Awww," she says.

We like Nita because she wears skin-tight tank tops and has a tattoo of Bart Simpson on her left shoulder. Some of us like her bright pink hair, some don't.

Spencer says: "Going to walk outside right now, find the nearest stroller, and punch the baby in it."

He starts to stand but he's hemmed in and nobody makes any effort to let him out of our horseshoe booth.

Marty says: "I'm going to kick a puppy."

I say: "I'm going to strangle an endangered species."

I say it for solidarity, even though, for the past two weeks, I've been flirting with a hot redhead from the plant who has no idea I'm already in a serious relationship. (I live with a beautiful young woman named Tanya Alvarez, who isn't here because she's in night school.)

The waitress comes and we order eggs, bacon, hash browns, toast, pancakes, extra butter, extra syrup, orange juice, coffee—a feast—because we're famished and because it's morning, technically. Saturday morning.

Nita says: "I wouldn't condone punching a baby."

"What if it's ugly?" Spencer asks.

"Maybe a baboon," she says. "I might punch a baboon."

"You're a terrible person."

"I have a baby," she says, "so I'm obligated to steer you in a different direction."

We know her mom looks after the kid (not really a baby anymore) so Nita can hold down a job and have a little fun once in a while. Like tonight. Nita is not in a hurry tonight. Everyone is asleep at this hour anyway, and we all need to come down from the pulse of Goo Goo Doll guitars still echoing through our brains.

"I never said YOUR baby."

"Fine, then. Whatever."

Nita clearly doesn't have the energy for this anymore.

"Line them up," Marty says. "I'm knocking them down."

WHERE WE LIVE

This is where we live.

El Camino Real, a.k.a. The Royal Road, a.k.a. The King's Highway.

Could be San Jose, Santa Clara, Sunnyvale, Mountain View, Palo Alto, Menlo Park ... El Camino connects them all.

Drive this road and you'll pass from one town to the next without even knowing it.

You'll see McDonald's, Taco Bell, TOGO'S, Pizza Hut, KFC and pretty soon you'll see them again.

You'll see dealers selling Fords, Toyotas, Jeeps, and BMWs.

You'll see Pet Smart, Toys R Us, Jiffy Lube, Walgreens, and BevMo.

You can rent a truck from U-HAUL, a car from Hertz, Avis, or Enterprise. You can stay in a Hilton or a Motel 6. You can get your hair cut, your car washed, your teeth fixed, your nails done, your laptop repaired.

If you don't see what you want, keep driving.

WOOD WORK

Monday comes too soon.

We punch in at 6 a.m. Twenty-minute break at 9:30. Forty-five minutes for lunch at noon. Off at 2:30, unless there's overtime, in which case we take a ten-minute break and work until 4:30.

We wear E*A*R plugs, spongy yellow cylinders we roll between our fingers. Once they compress, we jam them in our ears where they expand to block out the noise of all the panel saws, table saws, drill presses, and pin routers in the machine shop. The boards we cut and drill are used to make cabinets for kitchens and bathrooms, lockers for health spas, and other storage units for whatever the customer wants.

In addition to E*A*R plugs, we wear non-toxic particle masks, white bubbles that are held over the nose and mouth by a blue rubber band. They're custom-fitted by pinching the thin metal strip across the bridge of the nose. They keep most of the sawdust out of our lungs but sneezing is awkward.

Finally we wear a sort of welder's mask made of clear plastic. Often they're scratched up and hard to see through, but everyone wears one because it's no fun getting sawdust or a flying wood chip in your eye.

The main difference between a panel saw and a table saw is this: In the first the saw moves through the board. In the second the board moves through the saw. The panel saw has a huge table area and is used mainly for cutting huge sheets of plywood or pressboard. It's especially good, I guess, for making square corners, because the square corner is always marked with a pencil and stacked in a certain direction so that corner can be fed carefully into the table saw. You simply line the board up against the fence, as the guide is called, and feed it under the three red rubber wheels that pull it across the table and through the spinning blade.

We work in pairs, one person cutting, the other stacking, until a pallet is done and we trade places. But you have to be at least eighteen to operate a saw, so if you're paired with a seventeen-year-old you'll be sawing all day, which is more interesting but also more taxing. Most days now I work with Spencer, so it's not an issue for us.

There are air hoses by every saw and we use them frequently to blow away excess sawdust. There are also big vacuum pipes that suck up most of what falls under the saw. Water sometimes condenses in the air lines and you wind up spraying water on your table. That makes a sticky mess with the sawdust and you have to clean and wax the table. I never would have thought to put wax on a metal surface, but it works wonders.

A sign in one of the office windows says: "Measure twice, cut once."

Measurements are done with a floppy metal ruler called a scale. The scale divides each inch into tenths, hundredths, and thousands—and it's not unusual for specs to go three digits to the right of the decimal point. Tolerances—the allowable margin of error—are equally fine. That doesn't mean a board can be either a little small or a little large. Sometimes the tolerance goes only one way, and not too far at that.

The hard part for me is telling the difference between 12.67 and 12.68 or some such measurement. I stare at the scale and I try to focus and I'm never quite sure. Then I turn the two black knobs that tighten the fence and it moves a fraction. So I loosen them, bump the fence, tighten the knobs … loosen, bump, tighten … I'm finally learning to gauge how much the fence will move when I tighten it.

The foreman, Bob, makes his rounds, measuring twice, cutting once, and leaving us a sample to periodically compare our work to. If you bump the fence too hard you can knock it out of adjustment, or if you let too much sawdust accumulate next to it, your width will be off.

I don't tell people I have a college degree but Bob knows because it says so on my application. He shows me things, like how to set the blades to cut a dado or a rabbit. (A rabbit, in case you're wondering, is a lip cut into the side of a board and a dado is a groove cut further in.)

"OK, college boy," he'll say, "let's see how smart you are."

I always listen carefully and usually get it right.

"Atta boy," he'll say, and pat me on the back.

Bob is all right. He just likes to tease people. He can't keep a straight face, though, so you know right away he's just messing with you.

In the break area are six picnic tables, three on either side of the ping-pong table. There are pop and candy machines against the wall, and a drinking fountain with cold water. Coffee is free.

Most of the workers wear blue jeans, T-shirts, flannel shirts, and sweatshirts. Converse hightop basketball shoes are popular. Ninety percent of the guys have some kind of facial hair and would look better if they shaved it off.

During lunch, Marty generally joins a group of card sharks for few hands of Spades. Spencer and I sit together and shoot the shit with anyone who cares to join us.

He wants to be a chef and is taking classes at some sort of culinary academy; I want to be something, too, but I don't know what.

Nita works in the front office, where she doesn't really fit in with the others who are ten to twenty years older, so she generally has lunch with me and Spencer. (I think she has crush on him.)

I must admit I find one of Nita's office mates, Ariel Donatello, attractive enough to imagine myself boning her. She's the hot redhead I've flirted with a few times. Nita calls her a cougar and says all I'd have to do is say the word and she'd do me like there's no tomorrow.

Nita could be right.

But she also laughs when she sees me think about it. Like she can read my perverted mind. Not that I would actually cheat on Tanya.

HAPPILY?

We're all sitting at the Lakeside Café in Shoreline Park, drinking coffee and watching a lone windsurfer. This whole area used to be a garbage dump. Now it's a golf course and a man-made lake.

Marty tilts his head toward Spencer, and we all see that he's down in the dumps, as usual. We close our eyes and shake our heads, then return our attention to the struggling windsurfer.

Marty claps Spencer on the shoulder.

"Cheer up, dude," he says.

Spencer ignores him.

I look over at Tanya and she's not listening either. I wonder what she's thinking.

"Hey, I know," Marty says. "You want us to fix you up with a blind date?"

The windsurfer mounts his board, positions his sail, starts to move, loses his balance, falls back into the water.

"Nita, you've got a sister, don't you?"

"She's married."

For better or worse, there's not much wind on this sunny April morning. We sip our coffee and watch as our would-be surfer gets up, falls down, begins again.

Marty still thinks he could be on to something.

"Happily married?" he asks.

Nita laughs.

"No."

"Well, then?"

That gets her. She laughs so hard she starts to snort, which always embarrasses her. The kid likes it, though. She's got little Kayla with her today. The girl is so shy she will bury her face in her mother's side if you so much as look at her, but right now she's perched on a bright pink booster seat—same pink as Nita's bob—with nowhere to hide. We all do our best not to let her catch us looking at her.

"I'm sure Spencer could do a lot better," Nita says.

"Him? Are you kidding? He needs our help."

Spencer finally glances at us, clearly annoyed.

"Thanks a lot," he says.

Then he looks out at the lake again and so do we.

No doubt we're all thinking the same thing: More wind, please.

SERIOUSLY?

Tanya and I are at the Starbucks next to our apartment building. It's one of the last ones with overstuffed armchairs, and we're sitting in them, drinking tall mochas, while everyone else shifts uncomfortably in their hardwood counterparts. Tanya is wearing a black leather biker's jacket and a pretty polka dot dress—a look that I love—and I'm happy to have some time with her away from her business books.

She says, "I'm sorry, Luke, but I want you to move out."

"What? Why?"

Tanya shakes her head, then hooks her long black hair back behind her ears.

"A lot of reasons," she says. "Too many to name."

"Just give me one, then."

She sighs. A big heavy sigh, too.

"You don't take me seriously," she says.

"That's not true."

"It is, Luke. It is true. You know it is. You don't take anything seriously."

"So you shouldn't feel bad," I say.

She stares at me.

"I mean, if that's true, you shouldn't take it personally, right?"

She continues to stare at me. It does not feel good.

"This is really bad timing," I say.

"What would be a good time to break up?"

"I don't know," I say, "maybe when I was gainfully employed. You know, not ..."

"What?"

"Not the day I get laid off."

She looks me in the eyes.

"I'm not joking!" I say. "Me, Spencer, Marty ... We're all goners."

Tanya pries the plastic lid off her mocha, which I now realize is black coffee because, unlike me, she hates mocha. She takes a sip.

"I'm sorry," she says. "I had no idea."

"So I can stay?"

She shakes her head.

At first I think this is one of her semi-exasperated, what-am-I-going-to-do-with-you? head shakes. It isn't.

HOME AGAIN

My parents seem genuinely glad to see me when I turn up at their door, a little less glad when I ask if I can stay.

"Tanya and I broke up," I say by way of explanation.

We're in the kitchen and Mom is pouring me a glass of lemonade, with ice, because it's ninety-seven in the shade. She sets it on the counter and hugs me.

"Good," she says.

"Good?"

"She doesn't deserve you."

"Also, I lost my job."

Dad says, "Laid off?"

I nod.

"You'll find something better."

"For sure," I say.

Almost anything would be better.

Dad picks up the lemonade, takes a big gulp. I look at Mom.

"You want one, too?" she asks.

My old room is the new study, but my parents let me stay in the guest room, which is great.

I don't have a lot of stuff, just some clothes I bring over in two Hefty bags. All the stuff in the apartment—the bed, sofa, table and chairs, TV, books, and stereo—belong to Tanya.

Tanya is a serious person who has been busy collecting the essentials, the basics, and the nice-to-have items I tend to take for granted or simply do without.

I own some books—I'm not a cretin—but they're already (still) here, in boxes in the garage.

NEW JOBS

Spencer answers an ad offering training in European-style cooking and gets himself hired at this fancy eatery, Bistro 227, on Santana Row, home to a collection of upscale shops and restaurants in San Jose. He introduces me to Patrick, the sous-chef, who tells me they have an opening in pantry.

"Where's that?" I ask.

He points over his shoulder and goes on talking.

I'm thinking "Pantry" is a sister restaurant or maybe a small town I've never heard of. Finally I catch on. It's the part of the kitchen where salads, appetizers and desserts are assembled.

I agree to take the job and he puts me to work right away.

I change into the white uniform and hat the restaurant provides (in the closest approximation of my size I can find). The cooks all bring their own knives, and Patrick suggests I do the same, but there are a couple of beat up ten-inch chef's knives that belong to the bistro. He finds one and shows me how to sharpen it on a well-oiled sandstone block, then sets me to dicing onions.

Later, he shows me how to peel and devein prawns, skin and gut calamari, clean and crack crab ...

I like knowing how to do these things.

The kitchen is small and hot—up to 110 degrees on the line where Spencer works, grilling snapper, shark, sea bass, and sand dabs, but it's not so bad in pantry.

ALMOST HALF HUMAN

Spencer's car is in the shop, again, and he's trying to save enough money to buy something more dependable. I've never owned a car—I've always gotten around on my bike or the bus—but I figure it's time to get myself motorized. I've got my eye on a sweet Suzuki but haven't put enough aside yet.

In the meantime, Valley Transit gets us to our new jobs.

We get on the bus this one time and at first it's quiet, which is great because I, for one, feel like Jose Cuervo kicked me in the head with his blue agave boots. Then we hear this fat chick across the aisle talking to her skinny friend:

"She started sayin' a bunch a shit about Sherry, so I told her she'd better watch her fuckin' mouth 'cuz Sherry's my friend, but she kept on. So I told Sherry what she said. That bitch is gonna get her ass kicked if she don't shut up."

They get off at the next stop and it's quiet again for about half a block. Then there's this voice from clear in the back:

"I said, What, you gonna hit me again? Does it make you feel like a man?"

It's a woman on a flip phone.

"Ya see, I broke up with him," she says, "but he come beggin', come crawlin'. So I took him back. Then he hit me again. I said, That's the last time, boy, and I left."

The woman pulls the cord, the bus stops, and she gets off, still talking.

I close my eyes, rub my face, and try to hold my skull together. I'm pretty sure it has cracked somehow and I don't want my brain to ooze out. It's quiet for about thirty seconds, until we get to the next stop.

Two guys get on, one younger, one older. They sit across the aisle from each other, silent as monks, but then ...

"I don't go to school anymore," the kids says. "I'm too smart for school."

The older guy isn't sure he heard right.

"What's that?" he asks.

"I said I'm too smart."

"Too smart to go or too smart not to?"

"Too smart to go. They can't teach me anything."

The kid starts talking about this construction job he's got and all the money he's going to make. The older guy can't believe it.

"You think you're worth that much?"

"Sure I am. You should've seen me yesterday, climbin' on that roof. It was so steep I slid down, had to grab hold of the gutter. I was just hangin' there and started yellin'. They had to come put up a ladder so I could get down."

Spencer and I look at each other and shake our heads.

As we get off the bus, there's this grizzled old guy in a trench coat and a fresh-faced brunette in a floaty summer dress who's trying to get past all of us who have just flooded the sidewalk.

The old man says, "Hello, there, how are you?"

The girl glances at him, mumbles "OK," and tries to pick her way through the crowd.

"You're a real cutie, you know that?"

The old codger is grinning like a fool. We try to get out of the girl's way.

"You sure are a cutie."

She ignores his repeated praise and darts between Spencer and me.

"Well, go to hell," the old guy says. "I'm almost half human."

CHANCE MEETING

So it's Sunday afternoon and I'm hanging out at this place in Mountain View where Tanya and I used to hang—the café upstairs at Books Inc.

Tanya comes up the stairs, her thick black mane looking like she just got out of bed.

Damn! I love that look.

She's also wearing heels that make her legs look even longer, her butt even rounder.

I can't help but smile and I'm about to wave when I see there's this guy behind her and now he has his hand on her waist. There are flecks of gray in his short black hair and I can tell he's rich by the way his clothes fit and how soft they look.

I watch them order sandwiches and soup. He pays, of course.

Tanya starts to move in my direction and sees me sitting at what was always our favorite table. She flashes a quick half-smile and turns around, steers her new man in the opposite direction.

She needn't have bothered. I'm leaving.

HAPPINESS LOST

A hard mattress in a dark room.
    A dream of happiness lost.
    Wet sheets, cold air.

THE DINNER SHIFT

We work the dinner shift, which means we come in at three to get things ready.

I peel shrimp, clean calamari, tear lettuce, and boil pasta to a minute shy of perfection. Then I drain and cool the noodles before twisting them into single-serving bundles that I set into a tub, separating the layers with damp towels. Later, when an order comes in, all the cook has to do is grab a bundle, toss it into a wire basket, drop that into boiling water, and a minute later it's done. Just add sauce.

At four-thirty, the cooks sit down to eat in the dining room, a short break before the doors open at five.

Saturday night is the busiest.

Servers bring tickets to the sous chef, who calls out orders to the line cooks, starting with whatever will take the longest to cook and going down the list from there. Getting all dishes to a given table at the same time is impressive enough. Soon there are dozens of tables. (More than a hundred meals will be served over the course of the evening.)

I notice the chef has a collection of burns on his arms where he has reached into the oven too quickly and carelessly. He gets irate if plates sit too long before the server picks them up. Too long under the heating lamps and sauces get skins on them.

Servers also bring tickets to me over in pantry. I assemble salads and crab cocktails. I shuck oysters and clams and send them out on beds of crushed ice. I slice the cheesecake and scoop the gelato.

The last ticket comes in at ten o'clock. But nobody ever gets kicked out and diners sometimes stay as late as midnight. Meanwhile, we shut down the ovens, the grills, and the steam table, put everything away, and clean our stations. I have to wait in case any stragglers want dessert, but I can do that from the bar with the rest of the staff.

MESSED UP

The thing about me that's kind of screwed up is, well, I'm not unfriendly but …

I'm not that interested in meeting new people, either.

Except girls. I like girls.

Except when I don't.

Except when they want more from me than I can give them.

I don't like it when people expect things from me. Girl or guy—doesn't matter. Expectations are hell.

Don't get me wrong. I keep my word and all that. If I say I'll be there I'll be there. The expectations I'm talking about are unspoken. Which means maybe I don't even know about them, see?

I don't read minds.

Or maybe I know somehow but I never signed up for that—whatever it is.

Don't try to hold me to something I never agreed to in the first place. That's messed up.

IN AWE

It's a Sunday morning. Not much of a crowd has come into the restaurant for brunch. Spencer and I are standing at the omelet station, waiting for someone to come up and ask for one with a little of this and some of that. We also happen to be talking about one of the waitresses, Naomi, loud enough so she can't help but overhear us.

She's a sexy little thing. Dimples, perky breasts, nice round butt. She drops a fork and picks it up without bending her knees, which gives us more to talk about.

The next time she comes within ear shot, Spencer turns to me and says, "Yeah, but would you respect her in the morning?"

Naomi walks closer.

"You would not only respect me," she tells us, "you would be in awe."

HEARING THINGS

I take a second, part-time job at a bookstore because I really want that Suzuki. The store is in a shopping mall.

Malls are microcosms.

You get glimpses into all kinds of interactions—the sad, the insecure, the intimate—all the time.

You hear a man approach the woman who waters all the plants:

"Excuse me. I was wondering if I could speak to you a moment. I'm a widower who's forgotten how to approach women and basically what I wanted was to ask you out to dinner but I've forgotten how to do that. You're probably married, it seems like all the beautiful and intelligent women around here are married. I do basically the same thing you're doing. I'm a gardener. No chance, huh?"

"No, I'm married."

You hear two women coming out of a restaurant after lunch:

"She was so pretty I was embarrassed to look at her she was just so pretty."

"Oh, but, Linda, you have a hang up about that."

"I know I do."

"You really do."

"I know I do because you've pointed that out to me before."

You hear two other women in a bookstore:

"Oh, look, we could get *Test Your IQ*."

"Or we could get *Test Your Sex Appeal*."

"I'd rather test my IQ."

If, like me, you happen to work in the bookstore, you get drawn into conversations like this:

"Why don't you ask him? I bet he knows."

"Can I help you?"

"No, no, no."

"Yes, you can. It's not for me. My fiancé would like to know ... Where are your books about sex?"

"Right over here."

"Oh, good ... where?"

"What are you looking for?"

"Do you have any sex manuals?"

"Right here."

"Like *Joy of Sex*? Oh, there it is. Here it is, honey!"

"There you go, Brad. Now you'll know how to handle me on our wedding night."

I smile, say nothing. I just take it all in. All these random encounters. All the confusion and frailty. The clues. The hints. The almost-revealed secrets.

SPENCER HAS PLANS

We go in through the back door, past the dishwasher's station where dirty mixing bowls and scorched sauce pans are starting to stack up. The cooks are not yet wearing the hats they will have to put on once the doors open for lunch, and the radio is cranked up as high as it will go without distortion.

With a long wooden paddle, Patrick, the sous-chef, fishes a single strand of fettuccini from a cauldron of boiling water. Tasting it, he turns off the burner. The blue flame disappears.

"Luke, give me a hand with this, will you?"

I pick up a clean, dry towel to use as a potholder, and we lug the twenty-gallon cauldron to the nearest sink, where we drain off the water, careful to hold our faces back from the gush of steam we know is coming.

As we set the cauldron down, Spencer comes out of the changing room. He is holding the jacket he left here last night—his phone and wallet still in their respective pockets.

Lucky bastard.

"If I had done that, all my stuff would be gone," I tell him.

Standing on his toes, Patrick turns down the radio, an old Panasonic that sits on a shelf high above the sink.

"You left here in a hurry last night," he says. "What were you thinking?"

Spencer grins and shrugs. We know he left with Naomi, so we can guess what he was thinking.

"You guys working tonight?" Patrick asks.

I nod.

"You know I'd love to be here," Spencer says, "but I've got other plans."

As we head out the back door, I can hear the envy in Patrick's voice.

"I'll bet you do," he says.

BAD BOY THAT I AM

I figure the motorcycle will make me happy and it does at first.

It's a black and red beauty that I get from this guy on Craig's List. Only has seven hundred miles on it and runs great. The guy is clearly sad to see it go.

"My wife gives me the silent treatment every time I THINK about riding it," he tells me.

So now the bike is mine.

First thing I do is ride it hard on the backroads through the Santa Cruz Mountains to the beach. I've never felt so free.

I'm especially happy when Tanya sees me park it in downtown Mountain View. I can see her checking me out—sexy bad boy that I am. There's a ghost of a smile on her lips.

I take off my helmet and wink at her.

She's stunned.

I give her a nod and walk away—oh, yeah—cool as can be.

In retrospect, the wink bothers me. The wink may have been over the top. I should have smiled. Or not, I don't know.

HISTORY OF HEARTACHE

I dated quite a few girls in my school days. Short-lived relationships with long dry spells in between. I remember them all fondly now—Jennifer, Alison, Sydney, Zoe, Heather, Tara, Brittany, Carrie, Kirsten—even though most of them left me heartbroken.

I got myself into some sticky situations, too, hooking up with girls I had no real interest in; I was just lonely. I'm sure some of them hooked up with me for the same reason—they were hurting and needed me to lick their wounds—only I wasn't smart enough to see it at the time. Probably willful ignorance. I was always happier when I was with someone, even the wrong someone.

My problem was I took it all too seriously. I fared better when I lightened up. Sad to say, the ones I didn't take seriously, who I went out with just for kicks, are the ones I think the most of now. I didn't always treat them well, if you want to know the truth, but it was easier if they left me. Now I think I messed up some really sweet opportunities.

Mostly, though, I was smart enough to see when it wasn't going to work, and I would steer clear. Even if I was lonely. Mostly. I did say mostly. I don't want to sound like I'm contradicting myself, but I suppose I've often contradicted myself where women are concerned.

I won't be happy until I find The One.

I thought Tanya might be The One, and I was serious about her, no matter what she says. I was just trying to keep things light. My bad.

A LITTLE TASTE

Turns out we all like basketball, so we meet at this park over by the Pruneyard in Campbell to see who's got game. We're all decked out in our Converse hightops, Big Dog shorts, and mismatched T-shirts. Each of us brings a ball, too, which means we're knocking each other's shots out of the clear blue sky, all shooting at once. At first. Then we get wise.

Spencer shows up late, driving a rusted old Bel Air station wagon. We all give him shit for buying such a beater, but he says he got a good deal and they don't make 'em like that anymore.

"That thing will still be on the road when we're in our graves," he says.

Then he takes his first shot, a high-arcing twenty-foot jumper, and sinks it. Just like that. Nothing to it.

"Look at that!" Marty says. "He sure has his form down on that jumper, doesn't he?"

"He gets up there, too," I say. "He's got good springs."

"Wait a minute, you're not saying he gets up there higher than me, are you?"

"Well, Marty, his feet do leave the ground."

We all laugh.

"Hey," Marty says, "I have a bone to pick with you, Spencer. You said you weren't going out drinking last night."

"That's right. I didn't go out drinking."

"You weren't at home."

"I didn't say I was going straight home."

"Oh-ho, did Spencer go over to Naomi's again? I tell you, Spencer, you are the most pussy-whipped guy I've ever met."

"Oh, thank you very much. I just want you to know, Marty, that you are the most studly guy I've ever known."

"I can accept that."

Again, we all laugh.

"You know, Spence, you get a little taste and you turn into a puppy dog."

Spencer grins, drives left, pulls up, hits another jumper.

"You come out here and you're the big ball player."

"That's right. I come out here and kick your ass."

"Big ballplayer by day, puppy by night."

"What's wrong with that?"

HOOK UP

The Backstreet Bar & Grill is my kind of place. A funky little brew pub where you can get ale, porter, pilsner, lager—whatever you want.

The menu is a giant chalkboard listing a dozen kinds of sandwiches and a bunch of other stuff. Chili, nachos, beer-steamed hot dogs.

You order at the counter and they fix your sandwich (or whatever) while you wait. Then you seat yourself in a booth or table and wander over to the bar to pick up a pint.

If the weather is nice, you can take your stuff up on the roof. That's where Nita and I are on this unseasonably warm day in early May, waiting for the rest of the gang to arrive.

She wants to know if I've hooked up with Ariel yet. I tell her no.

"Yes you have," she says. "I know you have."

I shake my head.

"She tell you that?"

Nita sips her amber ale, wipes foam off her lips, and smiles at me.

"You women talk about everything, don't you?"

Her smile gets bigger. If she didn't know before, she knows now.

"Shit!"

"What's the big secret? Everybody knows she's been wanting to bag you for months. Why shouldn't you take a little comfort in those mongo boobs?"

This makes me laugh. Ariel, you may recall, is the older redhead from where I used to work and she does have spectacular tits. They're real, too.

"So, tell me," Nita says. "Is it true that her husband likes to watch?"

She says this as I'm trying to take a drink. Hefeweizen shoots out my nose.

"He doesn't even live there anymore," I say. "They're getting a divorce."

"That what she told you?"

"Ha ha, the place was emp..."

Nita looks doubtful.

"You're just messing with me now," I say. "Aren't you?"

PROUD

At the mall, a middle-aged woman returns a copy of a book she bought a few days earlier.

"My husband made me bring it back because we don't have a dog and we're not planning to get one, so I guess it is kind of stupid to have a book about training dogs," she says.

"Do you have your receipt?"

"No, I don't know what I did with it."

"I can give you a store credit," I say.

"Couldn't you just give me cash?

"Sorry, store policy."

"But it's only twenty dollars."

I shake my head.

"Fine," she says.

When she's gone, I mimic her entitled voice: "It's only twenty dollars."

My coworker, who heard the whole thing, says, "What about it?"

"To me, twenty bucks is twenty bucks."

"There's no reason to be snobby about it."

"Me? I thought she was the snobby one."

"But really you are in your own way. Your problem, Luke, is you're proud of being poor."

"Thanks for setting me straight."

"Somebody has to."

WAITING

A high-pitched voice screams something. A few short syllables. Totally unintelligible.

I am just coming over a wooden footbridge when I see them in front of me to the left: A young man with short black hair, dressed in gray sweatpants and a purple jacket (Marty), and a young woman, also with dark hair, who wears skinny jeans and a forest green hoodie (Jackie, I think her name is).

I'm here to play a little one-on-one with Marty, but he's clearly busy and I don't want to interrupt. I keep walking and watch through the corner of my eyes. He tries to grab her arm and she pulls away.

"No," she says.

I glance over and see her pushing on his chest with both fists.

"No."

I am past them now but I glance back to see Marty running. He carries a long navy duffel bag under his arm. As he reaches the crest of the arched bridge, he slows his pace enough to look over his shoulder (to see if she is chasing him?) and keeps going. He runs almost out of sight before slowing to a walk. He stops and looks back, then drops the bag on the grass and settles down beside it.

I don't think she can see him because of the bridge and the trees in the way, but he can see if she gets up from where she now sits cross-legged on the grass. I get the feeling he is just waiting to see what she will do.

I've got the ball and could go shoot some hoops on my own, but I circle behind the girl and find a seat on the other side of the knoll because now I'm curious.

Then I see Marty's head, his shoulders, his torso. He stops. His hand goes up as if he has just dropped something in front of her. (The duffel bag?) He spins around and his frame sinks out of sight.

I blink and he's back. His hand cuts the air horizontally in a gesture of finality. So I think, *That's it. He'll come find me now and we'll play some b-ball.* But when I walk back around, he is on one knee in front of her. Her head is down.

I hear her saying, "How do you know?"
And him saying, "Oh, boy . . . Oh, boy . . ."
He can't believe she is questioning him.

For a long time they just sit there. She won't even look up at him. If they're saying anything at all, it's pretty quiet. But all of a sudden he's on his feet again and stalking away. Then he runs back grabs the duffel bag and starts off once more. But once more, like a yo-yo on a short string, he's back, standing over her. He throws down the bag and slowly peels off his jacket.

"Here, you want this, too?"

(The bag must be hers or in some way "theirs" but certainly not his.)

He swings the jacket around once angrily while she, head still down, ducks even further. Calmly, it seems, he puts his arms back in the sleeves and raises them until the jacket slides down around him. He turns and trots across the bridge.

Instead of following the cement path this time, he turns sharply to his left and follows the dry creek bed, watching all the while to see if she will look up. She does not. She only drops her head lower between her legs, letting her hair fall down over her feet and hands.

Marty disappears into the creek bed and emerges on the other side. He walks slowly, keeping his eyes on the girl as he carefully steps over a bed of flowers. It doesn't matter what direction he chooses to sneak up on her, though, because she does not look up. Perhaps realizing this, he strides up to her.

She looks up and I can see her lips move, but her voice is quiet.

Marty squats in front of her on one knee. For about ten minutes they seem to be talking. Occasionally she even looks at him. He pops up, spins away, comes back, kneels. More talking. He pushes her down backwards. She resists, but he wins.

Because of the trees I can't see much. I shift my position for a better look and suddenly his fist is pounding—four quick blows. What is he hitting? The ground? The duffle? His own leg? Not her. She'd be screaming.

He lets her sit up and while he is apparently talking, she reaches out and tries to scoot the bag closer to her side. He gets up and walks slowly away, not across the bridge but in the opposite direction. I figure, *That's it. For sure. It's different this time because he didn't run.* But I'm wrong. He goes back to her, and after a brief exchange she goes with him, carrying her bag. I wonder what finally convinced her.

I guess he's forgotten all about meeting me here because they're going in the opposite direction from the basketball court. I should go shoot a few. I'm here. I have the ball. Instead, I follow at a distance.

I hear Marty saying, "Does that mean you want to go back to . . ."

Someone? Somewhere? I can't make out the end of the sentence.

"Is that what you want? Is it?"

The girl in the green hoodie sits on the grass again and mumbles something.

Marty says, "I can say Hi any time I want. Hi. Hi. Hi. Hi. Hi. I can say Hi any time I want."

I find another bench and wait. I really want to play some one-on-one.

GOOD FORTUNE

We're all clustered around one of the high round tables at Panda Express eating kung pao chicken and honey walnut shrimp, among other things. When we're done, we open our cellophane-wrapped fortune cookies.

"What does yours say?"

Nita reads: "You should enhance your feminine side at this time."

Marty says: "Hey, Spencer, Nita got your fortune."

Spencer forgets to laugh.

"If you dream it," he reads, "it will happen."

"False."

That's Marty, the eternal pessimist.

"It will happen," Naomi says, "if you make it happen."

Spencer shakes his head.

"To dream," he says, "is to court disappointment."

"Got that right, brother."

I'm not sure I agree, but then I'm not sure I disagree. I've been trying to land a teaching job ever since I graduated two years ago, but four hundred resumes later, I can't seem to make it happen.

An ambulance goes wailing by on Stevens Creek Boulevard. Nita waits for it to pass and then she says this: "I had a dream that I had a pet Dodo bird and we went skateboarding together in the park. Then, it happened."

THE NATURAL

Spencer Talbot is a natural. Smoothest jumpshot you'll ever see.

Some days it seems like everything he lets fly drops straight through the hoop. Nothing but net.

In high school, he tells me, he made the varsity team as a sophomore. But he took his gift for granted. Partied too much. Got arrested. Got kicked off the team.

He sat out his whole junior year, got a second chance as a senior.

Again he led the team in scoring. Again he threw it all away.

Driving while fucked up.

FORGET ABOUT IT

The bike makes me a loner, which is a cool persona, but kind of a drag, too. Nobody wants to hop on the back, you know? I've got nobody to share the thrill with me.

Nita would ride with me if her mother didn't object. Not that she always does what her mother tells her. Mama never liked the tattoo and doesn't care for the pink hair either, but the bike? Forget about it.

"You get on that bike, Nita, and that's it!" she says.

The rest of the conversation is in Chinese, but I get it. She doesn't want Nita to die. She doesn't want Kayla to grow up without her mother.

I'm about to tell her I'll be careful and drive slow, but as I start to open my mouth, the look she gives me makes me shut it fast.

The next day I put the bike on Craig's List. It sells within the week, helmet and leather jacket included.

THE REST ARE FOR ME

Naomi Torres is a hottie. We've established that, right? Dimples, perky breasts, nice round butt?

Lucky us. Lucky her. She can easily get what she wants.

When she was a teenager, she tells us, her parents got an unlisted number—and they wouldn't tell her what it was! Why not? Because they didn't want boys calling the house at all hours of the day and night.

"I was, like, fourteen, and I was a terrible flirt," she says. "I was always giving my number to cute boys, and there seemed to be an awful lot of them around in those days. Not like now.

"Hey, what's that supposed to mean?" Spencer asks.

"Now there's just you," she says. "Cutest boy on earth."

Spencer grins and puffs out his chest.

"Damn straight," he says.

A minute later Naomi is telling us that she masturbates once a day for the health benefits.

This is in a noisy pizza parlor in Mountain View. She isn't shy about speaking up and doesn't seem to notice when heads turn.

"The other four times," she tells us, "are just for me."

Not original, you say? Who cares? She's a hottie.

Marty, naturally, asks if she could use a hand.

Naomi just smiles and shakes her head.

Spencer slugs him in the shoulder.

BIGGER THAN THE REST

Marty Watson is bigger than the rest of us, but he wasn't always.

He started school early, which meant he was one of the smallest kids in his class, and he didn't have a significant growth spurt until near the end of high school. Then he shot up like six, seven, eight inches.

Kids who used to push him around had another thing coming. The new Marty worked out and didn't take shit from anybody.

His saving grace was that he didn't give shit, either.

Oh, sometimes you could tell he was just itching for someone to give him an excuse so he could settle old scores, but they wouldn't dare and that seemed to be satisfaction enough for Marty.

Still, the guy has a pretty short fuse, and I think he forgets how intimidating he can be at six-three, two hundred thirty pounds.

Lately he's gotten a bit, well, crude, and would probably benefit from a slap upside the head now and then. But who's going to do that?

On the other hand, he didn't retaliate when Spencer punched him.

HEAVEN ON EARTH

As I write this I'm watching the day disappear.

I'm thinking about the summer Tanya and I fell in love.

The summer I fell in love with her.

Back then, I was sure she loved me, too. But did she? Did she really?

We went camping in the High Sierra and swam every day in an icy alpine lake. I still get hard picturing her in her itty-bitty bikini, the lake water trying its best to cling to each and every one of her curves but slipping off with a silent sigh and lying at her feet, spent but satisfied to have had the chance to hold and caress her before evaporating in the sun, giving up heaven on earth for heaven above and gaining the chance to fall again.

USED CAR

I need a car now and like the looks of this old Scirocco. I offer the guy a few hundred less than he wants, a few hundred more than I have. He refuses at first, but I leave him my number and he calls me back the following week. Turns out he's moving out of the state in a U-Haul and doesn't want to tow the car.

To make up the difference I go to the Bank of Dad, where I know I can get favorable terms on a loan.

The car is silver with a black interior. For some reason I can never remember the year it was made, but it has a tape deck, so that should tell you something.

Still, it runs great.

NOT FUNNY

We're running a special on FRESH abalone and Naomi wants to know how much we have left.

Patrick says, "I've got thirty more pounds of it in the freezer."

Naomi shakes her head.

"Not funny," she says.

Our motto: We never serve frozen fish at Bistro 227; we thaw it first.

CLOSE ENCOUNTER

I'm shelving new arrivals in nonfiction and I can feel someone standing very close. I turn and, unavoidably, crash into her.

"Sorry," I say.

"I'm not," she says.

It's Ariel and she's smiling broadly.

"Oh," I say, as quick on my feet as ever. (I haven't seen her since that time we hooked up and I've been avoiding the bar where I ran into her.)

"So, this is where you landed."

"It pays the bills," I say. "Well, some of them."

I don't tell her about my other job.

Ariel shakes her head.

"You could do so much better," she says.

I shrug.

"It's a tough market."

She fingers her necklace, which draws my eyes to her breasts. Damn, it's hard to look away.

"I hear Nita's doing well," she says. "Finally got her break."

"With the magazine? Yeah, she's totally stoked."

It's an unpaid internship, but I'm not sure Ariel knows that.

"What would you do if you had the kind of support she's getting?"

So she knows Nita's mom encouraged her to quit her job, said she'd carry her for a while, let her get some experience in her field, maybe finally start to put her degree to work for her.

"My parents aren't exactly flush right now," I say.

They lost money in the market, which has meant Dad won't be able to retire any time soon. Hell, even my mom is looking for work.

"No, but what would you do?" she asks.

I don't answer because I don't know. I think I've contacted every school district in the state by now and my resolve to someday teach English is waning. Maybe I should have chosen another path, but what would that be?

"Well, think about it," Ariel says.

Is she offering to help me? Does she have that kind of money? (Her ex does own the woodworking plant where she met him and I met her.)

I smile uncertainly and she turns to leave.

Over her shoulder, she mouths the words, "Call me."

DISEASE-FIGHTING NEUROPEPTIDES

I'm totally surprised when Naomi calls me, midmorning, on my mobile. How, I wonder, does she even have my number?

"So," she says, "what are you up to, Luke?"

"I was trying to stimulate the production of disease-fighting neuropeptides."

"In other words, jacking off."

"Just doing my best to emulate your daily regimen."

"So you were thinking of me, then."

"I suppose you could say that."

"Do you often think of me when you masturbate?"

"Not really."

"No?"

"Just remembering your prescription for better health," I tell her.

"That's not really the same," she says, disappointed. "Next time I want you to think of me. Will you?"

"Uh, I guess ..."

"Promise me."

"Seriously?"

"Pretend it's me stroking your bone," she says. "You have to take off all your clothes, though, because that's what I'd do. I'd strip you naked first."

"I have to go now," I say.

She laughs and hangs up. I have no idea why she called. In the coming days I'll begin to wonder if this conversation even took place.

LIFE

This is all pretty random, isn't it?

LIKE WATER

People tell me I need to take charge of my life.

I get it.

So far I've kind of just let my life happen to me.

But you know what? Overall, I'm pretty happy with how it's been going. I'm not sure my trying to take charge would have changed a hell of a lot. Maybe it would have made things worse, who knows?

I like to go with the flow. Not that I would just go along with something I think is wrong. I wouldn't do that. But I'm generally happy to eat at whatever restaurant you like, see any movie you want to see. Well, pretty much. Not one of those *Jackass* movies.

Always trying to get your way isn't going to make you happy as far as I can see.

Also, I've never liked goals and deadlines. I mean, if I want to do something, I'll do it. If it's important, I'll get it done. Otherwise ...

Aren't we supposed to live in the now? Isn't that what all the gurus say? Key to happiness and all that.

So give me a break, OK?

I do what I can.

SOMEONE ELSE

In downtown Mountain View, Castro Street is lined with restaurants—Chinese, Italian, Mexican, you name it. Many of them have tables on the sidewalks, which is where I spot Naomi. She's sipping a glass of red wine and gazing off into the distance. I stop, casting a shadow across her table, but she doesn't notice.

"I might have known I'd find you guys here."

Finally, she looks up.

"Luke! How are you?"

She's wearing a short yellow dress and looks fantastic, as usual, her bare legs crossed and on display like works of art.

"Spencer in the boys room or what?"

"I don't know where he is."

"He just wander off? He does that sometimes. Must have forgotten to take his meds."

Naomi smiles at my joke.

"No, he's not with me."

"Oh, I thought ..."

I look at the half-empty glass across from her.

"I'm here with a friend," she says.

"Is she cute?"

"What?"

"Do I want to hang around and meet her?"

I start to sit. Naomi shakes her head. I stand back up.

"That bad, huh?"

"Not your type, I shouldn't think."

Then I see this dude behind me. Tall, handsome, well-dressed.

"Luke, this is Jason. Jason, Luke."

We shake hands and look at each other quizzically but Naomi offers no details to either of us. I decide not to ask.

"Well, I should be going," I say. "Nice to meet you, Jason."

TELLING

I don't know whether I should tell Spencer about the encounter but I do. I mention it as casually as I can. The implication is clear enough, though. Or maybe not.

"So," he says, "what are you saying?"

"I'm saying I ran into Naomi today."

"Naomi and this guy?"

"Yeah."

"Jason?"

"Yeah."

"Who is he?"

"No idea."

"Who did she say he was?"

"That's just it. She didn't."

"Are you trying to tell me something, Luke?"

"No, just ... what I said."

THE HOUSE IN SUNNYVALE

Spencer is telling me about this house in Sunnyvale, partially furnished, that we could rent if we go in together.

"The old tenants just moved out," he says. "I know the landlord, so we're first in line."

"How much?"

"How much can you afford?"

"What kind of question is that? Same as you," I say. "Unless you want to pay more."

"I want the master bedroom so, yeah, I'll pay a little more ..."

That's when Marty shows up. He wants to know if there's room in the house for him.

"It's two bedrooms," Spencer says, "and I'm not sharing."

Marty looks at me. I shake my head.

"Come on, man," he says. "You know what rents are like with all the ones and zeros out there."

"Ones and zeros?"

"Yeah, you know, the coders. The big-bucks brainiacs. The Googlers and Twits."

That's when Spencer says, "The room actually has bunk beds."

I wonder when he was going to tell me that.

Marty and I work out a deal that I already know I'm going to regret. We move in on the first of June.

RUNAROUND

The house is small—two bedrooms, one bath—and poorly insulated. Built in the 1950s, it has a tar-and-gravel roof, single-pane windows with aluminum frames, and two gas-powered wall heaters you can turn on or off. There is no thermostat. Still, it's a house, not an apartment.

I find Spencer in the living room with Naomi when I get home from work. (They both had the day off and the place smells of weed and tunafish.)

Spencer says, "Dude, I think you owe Naomi an apology."

"I do? Why?"

"For telling Spencer I was fooling around on him," she says, leaning back, crossing her legs, and staring at me through slitted eyes.

"I never said that."

"No? What did you say?"

"I said I saw you in town, with that guy ... what's his name?"

"Jason?"

"Yeah, Jason. I said I ran into you and Jason."

"And?"

"And nothing. I saw you and I mentioned I saw you."

"You weren't trying to suggest ..."

"No, I swear."

I'm lying now and Spencer knows it, but he lets me off the hook.

"Relax, dude, we're just messing with you."

Now they can barely contain themselves.

Spencer says, "You should have seen the look on your face, man."

Naomi is smiling but hasn't finished teasing me.

"Who did you think Jason was?"

"No idea," I say. "Who is he?"

"My brother."

"You have a brother?"

"He lives in Boston," she says. "He was out here on business."

"Oh," I say.

They both bust up laughing.

DAY IN THE LIFE

Spencer and I have different days off, which is probably a good thing. We see enough of each other at work and home. Marty is on a different schedule altogether. I don't know what he does with his time. I hope he's out there hunting for a job.

I look forward to my days off, but then, sometimes, I don't know what to do with myself. Some days I head over to the park to see if I can get into a pick-up game; other days I just don't have the energy. Some days I drive to the beach; other days I can't afford the gas.

I used to visit my mom and dad at least once a week, but that's a little trickier than it used to be. Mom has been picking up temp jobs, so I'm never sure if she's going to be home. My dad continues to work in Facilities for one of the valley's high-tech giants—a lot of his time is spent reconfiguring cubicles and moving computers and phones from place to place as the company continually reorganizes itself—and he has tons of crazy stories to tell about so-called corporate efficiency.

I know he's always glad to see me, but I feel bad because I have yet to start paying him back for the car loan. Not that he'd ever say anything (Bank of Dad offers exceptionally lenient terms) but I feel like such a deadbeat.

Today I sleep late, shower, masturbate, shave, masturbate, eat a bowl of cereal, masturbate. Life is good, but I need to figure out how to make it better before I go blind.

A DRIED WHITE SUBSTANCE

Naomi shares a story about the chef de cuisine—the guy in charge of the menu—where we work:

"Some snake face came into the restaurant one night and Vince took her up to the office and screwed her on the couch," she says. "Next day the owner is sitting on the couch and notices a dried white substance on the leather."

We all make disgusted faces.

"He scrapes it off with his fingernail and says, 'Who's been eating chowder up here?'"

CLASS WARFARE

On the beach in Santa Cruz, not far from the Boardwalk, we all huddle around our little driftwood bonfire. We drink Budweiser, the King of Beers, from long-necked bottles and stare into the flames. The sun went down hours ago.

"What the fuck is wrong with this country?" Spencer wants to know.

"Everybody's scared," I say.

"Scared of what? Terrorists?"

"Forget terrorists. People are scared of losing what they've got."

"If they've got anything," Nita adds.

"Yeah," Naomi says, "they're afraid we're going to rise up and take our share."

Spencer pokes the fire with a stick, says: "We should, too, you know."

"Right on, brother. Class warfare. I'm in."

That would be Marty. I ask if he's going to occupy Wall Street.

"Hell, no, I say we raid the place. Steal from the stealers."

"Right. We can abscond with all their mortgage-backed securities."

"No, Luke, those we stuff up their bungholes."

"Mmm, good place for them."

"Right back where they came from, my friend."

"So what do we steal?"

"We steal their identities, man. No one will touch us if we're them."

"Cayman Islands, here we come."

The wind is blowing now, bringing in clouds that block out the moon. I've already eaten three hot dogs but start to roast a fourth.

"Why not? You think those Wall Street bastards deserve their bailouts and bonuses?"

Naomi finishes her beer and throws the bottle at our bonfire. It doesn't break, though. I think we're all disappointed.

"They don't even do anything real," she says.

"Got that right," Marty says. "Wall Street is one big casino, and the house always wins."

"Where else can you get million dollar bonuses for driving the whole country into the ground?" I ask.

"It's not just Wall Street," Naomi says. "It takes us a month—at least—to make what the average CEO makes in one hour. One fucking hour. You think those jackasses work four hundred times harder than we do? You think they're four hundred times smarter?"

Nita zips up her jacket.

"Here's what I don't get," she says. "If they're so smart, why are they all such miserable pricks?"

MISSING IN ACTION

Remember when every mall had a bookstore? Now it's rare. Now whole towns don't have one.

Bad news for book lovers. Bad news for me. My part-time gig has vanished behind butcher-papered windows.

I'll miss the extra income and the hefty discount on Longmire mysteries.

FUNNY MAN

The house is small and there's only one bathroom.

This is a problem.

Marty takes long showers with the door locked.

"Can't a guy get a few minutes to himself?" he says.

But it's not a few minutes. It's half an hour or more.

"You getting clean in there?" Spencer asks through the door. "Or getting dirty?"

"Funny man," Marty says.

This goes on for weeks and it's still funny.

The trick, of course, is to get in there before Marty does.

SECRET RECIPE

Naomi comes to the counter and calls Spencer over.

"I have a customer who wants to know the secret of our spaghetti sauce," she says. "What gives it its sweetness?"

"Sugar."

"Really?"

"Yeah, there's a tiny bit of sugar in the recipe."

"I'm not telling him that."

Spencer shrugs.

"I'm telling him you refused to reveal the secret."

GARDEN PARTY

Smoke from the barbecue swirls around the backyard in a shifting breeze.

Nita breathes it in.

"Don't you just love it?" she asks.

I nod.

"It's one of my favorite smells," she says.

"Mine too."

"Right up there with fresh baked bread and wet pine needles."

"Hmm, to me, nothing beats the smell of freshly ground coffee beans," I say, "and bacon sizzling in a pan."

"That your way of inviting me to stay for breakfast?"

"If you don't mind sharing the top bunk with me."

"Or you could share the bottom bunk with me."

This generous offer comes from Marty, of course. Nita swallows the last of her rum and Coke, holds up her empty tumbler.

"Couple more of these and I may take you up on that."

It's not entirely clear which one of us she's referring to.

Naomi says, "Spencer has a king-size bed. I think you'd be more comfortable with us."

"Plenty of room," Spencer says.

He flips burgers on the Weber and grins. Nita smiles back at him and Naomi. Such a tease. Almost as bad as Naomi herself.

Marty and I look at each other and shake our heads. They just say shit like that because they know what it does to our perverted minds.

All the same, I take Nita's glass and mix another drink for her.

ARIEL'S APPEAL

A big part of Ariel's appeal is she knows what she wants.

She knows and lets you know.

You don't have to guess.

You don't have to try to decipher subtle clues; the clues are obvious.

She might open with something like: "You're cute. I could eat you up."

If you look surprised by some risque remark she makes, she will lean in close and whisper in your ear: "Women like sex, too, you know."

Her hand will be on your thigh as she tells you this.

She may suggest you're too drunk to drive and offer you a lift.

In the car she'll get you talking about yourself—she's a good listener—and the next thing you know you're pulling into the driveway of her house in Los Altos. This will surprise her.

"Sorry," she'll say. "I must have been on autopilot. Well, as long as we're here you might as well come in and I'll suck you off ... I mean, fix you a drink."

INTO THE CROWD

Naomi shares a quote someone shared with her:

"Just about everyone, at some time in their lives, feels like walking into a crowd with a machine gun and just opening fire at about waist level, and anyone who hasn't had that feeling deserves a place in that crowd."

She can't remember who said it or who shared it with her, but she wants to know how she can get her hands on a machine gun. All because Vince tells her she'll have to put in a full year before she can qualify for a raise.

Owner's policy, he says. No exceptions. Nothing he can do about it.

ALL OUT

I hear Marty banging around in our funky blue and yellow kitchen, muttering and cursing. I'm stretched out on the sofa, watching a steady stream of Family Guy reruns on the ancient Trinitron that came with all the other furnishings in the house. I don't want to get up, so I just yell:

"What's the matter, big guy?"

"We're out of beer."

"No way."

"Way."

I get up, grudgingly, and go into the kitchen.

"I bought a six pack yesterday," I tell him.

Marty shrugs. I look in the fridge.

"What the fuck, Marty?"

"Must have been that bastard Spencer."

I fold my arms.

"Spencer? Really?"

"I'm telling you, that dawg can really put away the brewskis."

All I can do is shake my head.

"I didn't have a single bottle of my own beer."

"Buy a case next time," he says. "It's cheaper that way."

SWEETNESS

Turns out Nita lives on the same street as us, just two blocks south. Sometimes I see her on the front porch, sitting in an old-fashioned swing with Kayla, so I'll stop and chat with them.

"Need anything from the store?" I'll say, because I'm always on my way to the corner grocery.

Kayla, no longer shy with me, wants candy. She knows I'm a soft touch.

Nita usually says no, but sometimes I get candy anyway. Something we can share. Almond Joy is perfect because it comes in two sections.

I get two so Nita and her mom can share the other one. Her mom rarely comes out on the porch, though. She has yet to warm up to me.

"As of tomorrow I have only had one cigarette in two weeks," Nita tells me. "That one was only because I was soooo mad at my ex."

"Why? What did he do?"

"Nothing. That's the problem. He's supposed to ..."

She stops because she doesn't want to dis Kayla's father in front of her. I nod. This is the first time she's talked about him, but I get it. He's a jerk and she's pissed.

"How long were you married?"

"Oh, god, a long, loooong time," she says. "It must have been two months or more."

GOOD THING GONE

I was with Tanya for two years. I thought we had a good thing going. I even thought we might get married at some point.

I see now that it was never going to work.

I was just some guy she was with while she waited for someone better to come along. Someone serious. Someone who could take her out to dinner and never look at the right side of the menu.

I wonder if she's happy now.

I miss her.

THAT MISCHIEVOUS SMILE

We're at a party for Naomi's roommate, who is celebrating her twenty-fourth birthday. In the hallway outside the bathroom, I notice a picture on the wall. It shows a young girl, maybe ten or eleven, with a mischievous smile.

I look around the corner and catch Naomi's eye.

"Oh, my god," I say. "This is you, isn't it?"

She comes closer.

"Yup, me and Peter."

"Peter?"

"My brother."

"You have two brothers?"

"No, just the one is more than enough," she says.

"I thought his name was Jason."

I see Naomi's face change.

"You introduced him to me as Jason," I say.

"No," she says. "Peter."

"I remember distinctly…"

Her shoulders drop and she takes a deep breath.

"OK, look, I lied, all right? I made a mistake and I lied and I'm sorry," she says. "Don't tell Spencer. Please?"

I shake my head slowly.

"I am such a sucker. You played me."

"That was all Spencer's idea. He wanted to have a little fun with you."

"Oh, but you REALLY played me. I felt like such a jerk."

"I'm sorry. Really sorry. I had to make it real."

"So who is Jason?"

"An old friend. Doesn't matter. Just ... please?"

A FIRST FOR NITA

Nita's first article, a review of a local eatery, has just been published. To celebrate, we all go there and pass the story around while we wait for our food:

The Perfect Blend

I keep coming back to the Perfect Blend for the beef stroganoff. They do some nice things with veal and chicken here, but the stroganoff is what I usually order. It's more mushroom than beef, really, but that's OK because I like mushrooms, and the sauce is just right. I have mine over rice, but you can have noodles if you like.

The place is low-key and unpretentious. You pick up a menu on your way in and seat yourself. The tables are all small squares of laminated wood, and more often than not you can get one by the row of windows facing the fountain outside. It's not much of a fountain, if you want to know the truth, but the sound of cascading water is always pleasant.

As you might guess from the name, the Perfect Blend is designed to drive coffee lovers to distraction. They have something like forty-two kinds of coffee here, made only from arabica beans, which, I gather, are the best you can get. I always have the mocha-java borgia after dinner. It comes with a mound of whipped cream and a sprinkling of orange zest. Perfect.
—ANITA CHAN

"I like your style," I say.

She smiles and I'd kind of like to hug her. Maybe if we weren't sitting across from each other. I've never been friends with a girl before, so I don't know what's appropriate. I know this, though: I'm as happy as if her success were mine.

WASTED

Marty never seems to have any money (though he's working now, part time, slinging espresso drinks for a local coffee-roasting company), but he always has weed.

Spencer buys from him, and sometimes we all share a joint. It's nice, but then all I want to do is make a tuna sandwich or, better yet, a tuna melt. Either that or bake brownies, with walnuts if we have any.

I always feel stupid afterward. Like what am I doing with my life? (It doesn't help that I've received responses from three more school districts informing me that they WISH they could hire more teachers. Instead, they've had to let some go. Budget cuts, don't you know?)

Marty tells me to lighten up. Marty. The guy who is always up for a little class warfare or whatever.

Spencer is more philosophical.

"Time you choose to waste is not wasted time," he says.

I'm impressed until he tells me he saw it on Facebook.

Even worse, this will become Marty's favorite saying, only he will change it to: "Don't waste your time not being wasted."

ONE FOR THE SPANK BANK

I'm the first to arrive at the Backstreet Bar. Then Naomi. We get a booth in the back.

Naomi is wearing a V-necked sweater so loose it leaves one shoulder exposed. No bra strap. The material is stretchy enough that she can, and does, expose one breast as well. Just a little tug is all it takes. I watch, wide-eyed, as her nipple hardens. Then she covers it back up.

I look at her quizzically; she simply smiles.

"Just a little something for you to put in the spank bank," she says.

"Do it again," I say, fumbling for my phone. "I'd like to get a picture."

Naomi shakes her head, looks up and smiles. Spencer, Marty, and Nita are all coming toward us.

"What have we missed?" Spencer says.

CRASH

Monday we learn that one of our cooks has died in a car crash. His name was Chaun, and he worked the lunch shift. I didn't know him well but he was one of those guys here working at two restaurants and trying to get ahead. His house, I hear, was already mostly paid for even though I'd place him in his mid-thirties.

Now he's dead. Ran his Dodge Charger head-on into a flatbed truck loaded with bell peppers. He and his wife were burned beyond recognition.

At work everyone knew right away that something was wrong because he had never been late in seven years.

There had been footage of the aftermath on TV, but I didn't see it and even those who did never made the connection.

People who knew him agreed he tended to drive too fast, and some wondered if he fell asleep at the wheel. He had left L.A. at 1 a.m., crashed on Pacheco Pass at 7 a.m.

The news gives us all pause.

Here was a guy who worked hard for a future he and his wife will never see.

RENT

Marty disappears for a couple of weeks, without notice, then shows up again.

"You owe me," I say.

"Why's that?

"Rent."

"Oh, right, forgot about that."

"Where were you anyway?"

"L.A., mostly," he says. "Me and Fredson. Little road trip."

"Who's Fredson?"

"You know, guy we shot pool with that night at the Backstreet Bar."

"Right."

I don't remember him at all.

"He was driving down there and asked me to go along," Marty says. "Always wanted to see Disneyland and all that."

"Must be nice."

"Yeah, well ... Listen," he says, "I'm just going to pay half this time."

"What do you mean, half?"

"I wasn't here, so ..."

"So what?"

"So I'll just pay for the time I was here."

"It doesn't work that way, Marty."

"Why not? You had the place to yourself, so I figure ..."

"Look, you rent a hotel room they don't give you a discount for the times you aren't there. They're holding the room for you, so you pay for the whole time."

"Dude, this ain't no hotel."

"No, but you want a place to come back to, you pay your share."

"You want me out of here, just say the word."

"Come on, man ..."

"I can pay half," he says. "I got no job, remember?"

"Yet you can head down to L.A. and ..."

"That was all Fredson, man. He knew I wasn't doing anything and he wanted some company."

"Right."

Marty hands me some cash. It isn't enough, but I take it.

MIXED EMOTIONS

It's late, almost closing time, and I'm sitting here at the Backstreet Bar with Spencer because he likes to come here after work.

The problem with this place is that there's always a chance we'll run into Ariel. She gets that I've cooled toward her and that makes it awkward. Right now she's hitting on a guy who's even younger than I am. I try not to pay any attention but every now and then I happen to glance over there. Every time I do, she catches my eye. It's uncanny. She must think I'm watching her.

Maybe she thinks I'm jealous, I don't know. The look in her eye seems to say, *This could be you.*

I know the guy is in for a good time and that's fine.

The thing is, Ariel likes this place as much as I do, and neither one of us is ready to cede it to the other.

Shortly after midnight, she and her boy toy get up and make their way toward the door, grinning and leaning into each other. I reach out and grab

Ariel's forearm. She stops and looks at me, surprised, pleased, uncertain.

I nod toward their table and she sees her handbag there.

"Thank you," she says, but I get the feeling she would have been happier to leave it behind, credit cards and all, than to have to walk back and get it now.

THE WIND

The wind is blowing and I step outside just to feel it on my face. On the horizon, far away, fireworks flash. It's Independence Day.

BEST THING EVER

I get to the club about half an hour before the doors are supposed to open and already the line goes halfway around the block. Up ahead I see this girl looking right at me. She's bouncing up and down and waving, first with one hand, then both. Finally it dawns on me: It's Nita. I didn't recognize her at first because her hair is now blue—her third color in as many months. Spencer is with her and Naomi and Marty and his new friend, Fredson. That's his last name but that's what we call him. I don't know why. But I don't know why we do half the things we do.

We're here to see this new band from L.A. that Nita really likes, and when we get inside we grab a table near the stage. I notice Tanya and her new guy a few tables over but pretend not to see them. We all pretend.

"First round is on me," I say.

I head for the bar, knowing it will be way faster than waiting for table service. Not that the bar isn't already surrounded by suckers who have the same idea. Still, I manage to get my order in and I'm waiting patiently when this guy bumps past me and grabs this other guy by the shirt.

"You say something to Pam?" he wants to know. "How come she don't come around no more? How come she won't talk to me?"

Then this third guy steps in to break them apart. He's huge and I think he must be the bouncer, but then he says: "That's the best thing ever happened to you in case you don't know, you dumb shit."

I feel a hand on my elbow.

"Hear that, Luke?"

It's Nita.

"Best thing ever," she says.

She knows how I feel about Tanya but thinks I'm better off without her. I'm not so sure, but she's smiling so I smile, too.

"What are you doing?" I ask.

"I figured you could use a hand," she says and helps me carry the beers.

Nita leads the way, picking a path between the tables, her pleated skirt swaying, and I'm right behind her.

"I take it you never liked Tanya," I say.

"Oh, I liked her just fine."

"Then how am I better off?"

She has to stop to let someone pass and I bump into her from behind.

"Sorry."

"No problem."

We're walking again and I repeat my question.

"I just think you'd be happier with someone else," she says.

An hour later the band still hasn't taken the stage, so Spencer excuses himself to hit the men's room. Nita watches him walk away, then turns to Naomi.

"How did you two get together?" she asks.

"We met and work."

"And?"

"And I got tired of waiting around for him to make a move, so I clubbed him over the head and dragged him back to my cave."

Nita says, "I might have guessed."

"Why are the cute ones always so shy?"

"I know, right?"

Nita smiles, sits back, and looks at me. I don't know why. I'm not cute and I'm not shy. Not really. Not especially. Though anyone who's been burned has a right to be a little shy.

The band is upbeat and energetic. You can tell they love making music. Afterward we thank Nita and start to split up, having all parked in different directions. I make sure Nita gets to her car and is OK to drive.

"I had like one beer," she tells me.

Which is kind of funny because the club has a two-drink minimum.

I ask her if she's sorry she didn't make a move on Spencer before Naomi came along and she acts like she doesn't know what I'm talking about.

"I've seen the way you look at him when he's walking away."

"You've noticed that, huh? How come you've never noticed how I look at you?"

UM, OK

So I'm peeling and deveining twenty pounds of prawns in the back half of the kitchen near the walk-in coolers when my phone rings. I almost don't know what to do. No one ever calls me.

I look at the screen and see it's Tanya. I figure she must have butt-dialed my number, but ...

"We should get together," she says.

I say, "Um, OK."

"How about dinner, my treat?"

"Um, OK."

She suggests a time and place. I scrounge up a scrap of paper and a pencil and write it down.

"It's a date," I say. "Or whatever."

I don't know why she wants to see me. Maybe she broke up with that clown I saw her with. Maybe I owe her money. Maybe she's finally figured out I stole her favorite turquoise panties when I moved out.

I really hope that's not it.

"See you then," she says.

I say, "OK, um ..."

But she's already gone.

GETTING TO KNOW NITA

Nita Chan looks a lot younger than she really is.

She looks mid-twenties; she is mid-thirties.

She looks young and feels young (most of the time) and hangs with a young crowd. So sometimes she lies about her age. Mostly, though, she just lets people's assumptions stand.

There's a general prohibition against asking a woman her age, so that helps.

People assume she got pregnant in high school. Nita lets them believe that. Actually she already had her bachelor's degree in communications, a field she is only now breaking into.

Nita tells me the truth because she believes the punishment for lying is always wondering if others are lying to you.

She also believes this: If you like to dance, dance—and don't let anything stop you. Not shyness. Not anything.

So we're dancing, not in a club or a bar, but in her living room, with Kayla, who is not shy at all, not here, not with us.

Kayla thinks I'm funny. Nita's mother isn't sure what she thinks.

TOGETHER AGAIN

Tanya smiles and we hug.

"You look great," I say.

I can't help it, she does.

She thanks me with a gentle touch on the arm.

The hostess seats us right away, on the patio, under the shade of a big red umbrella.

"The burgers here are awesome," Tanya tells me.

She knows what I like.

We talk about our search for the perfect burger and how each place we found eventually closed, sending us off to renew our quest.

"Could this be the one? The new one?"

Tanya curls her lower lip and shrugs.

"Maybe," she says.

I wonder if that's why she invited me here—to share her find and confirm its superiority over all others—but she doesn't give me time to ask.

"So," she says, "how are you?"

I tell her about my new job and the house in Sunnyvale, my issues with Marty. She laughs and so do I because now it seems funny to me. It didn't before.

And that's how it goes. We talk and eat our burgers (they are damn good, but maybe not the best) and then we part on the sidewalk with another brief hug.

ONE OF HER MOODS

Spencer and I are sitting on white plastic lawn chairs in the backyard with the last two bottles of Bud from the fridge. I don't know where Marty is. Working, maybe, or hanging with his pal, Fredson (who is not, I suspect, a good influence).

"I thought you'd be over at Naomi's place," I say.

"She's in one of her moods."

"I thought she was always in the mood."

"Not that kind of mood," Spencer says. "She's depressed."

"Really? Why?"

"Ask her. She'll give you a million reasons."

"I find that hard to believe. A girl like her."

"You don't know her like I do," he says. "She gets totally down on herself sometimes. Hates her job. Hates her apartment. Hates her roommate. Hates herself."

"She needs you to go cheer her up."

"Right. She gets like this, there's nothing anyone can do."

I say, "I bet you could."

"Dude, I just talked to her. She complained about everything. I couldn't get off the phone fast enough."

Spencer kicks back, takes a long pull from his bottle.

"She was really bringing me down," he says. "I don't think I'll be calling her for a while."

WHAT HAPPENS NOW?

I keep thinking how great it was to see Tanya again. I didn't think she'd be so easy to talk to. Like old times.

But, really, what was that all about? What happens now? Am I supposed to call her, ask her to go out again? I think about it every day, every time I have a break.

I take out my phone, and I put it back in my pocket.

Don't be too eager.

Don't be a fool.

Don't get your hopes up.

Stop! Just do it. Just call her already.

No. No. She'll break my heart.

Coward!

Then I find the fancy square envelope in our mailbox. There's an embossed card inside and gold letters requesting the honor of my presence as Tanya Alvarez and Trevor McKesson pledge their love to each other or some such horse shit.

STRAWBERRY RHUBARB

The refrigerator is empty, as usual, so I head over to Marie Callender's on El Camino. Instead of sitting at the counter and ordering a slice of my favorite strawberry rhubarb pie—something I do when I want to treat myself—I get a whole one and take it back to the house.

Everybody else is still in bed.

I cut myself an extra big slice. Call it breakfast.

Damn! That Marie makes a flaky crust.

I decide I'll have another slice and then I remember what happens to pie (beer, corn flakes, bread, eggs, milk) in this house.

You see where this is going, don't you?

That's right, I'm eating this whole pie in one sitting.

Fuck you, Marty Watson! Fuck you, Spencer Talbot!

I don't even want the last piece but I eat it anyway.

I do not feel proud of myself.

Then I stretch out on the sofa and take a nap. It's 9 a.m.

HORSE SHIT

My mom is not working today so we're able to have one of our kitchen conversations where she imparts her unique brand of wisdom. She assures me that, no matter what I may think now, a wedding invitation is not horse shit.

"You should feel flattered," she says. "The fact that Tanya wanted to have dinner with you means she needed to be sure."

"And now she is. Great."

"Look, I did the same thing before I married your father. I still remember the boy fondly, even now. It's been forty years and I still think about him sometimes."

I still don't get how all this is supposed to perk me up, and I guess my mother can see that. She gets up, pours herself another cup of coffee, and offers me more as well.

"I've had enough," I say.

She looks at me and shakes her head the way she often does. Then she has another thought.

"Don't tell your father," she says.

CHUMP CITY

I am the mayor of Chump City.

NITA'S EX

I ask Nita about her ex and this is what she tells me:

He was this happy-go-lucky guy when we met. Kind of shy. A little awkward. I always liked that.

He would say, "Let's get high," so we would.

I liked weed back then. Now, not so much.

So, anyway, it was this social thing. We'd get high together or with some of our friends. Whoever we were with when he'd say, "I know, let's get high."

It wasn't about escaping our stupid lives or easing some gnawing existential emptiness. Not at first. And it never was for me, but it was different for Ben.

After a while he didn't want to go out anymore.

"Let's just stay in," he'd say.

I knew what that meant. It meant let's get high by ourselves. More for each of us.

I started saying no.

He'd shrug and light up.

"Suit yourself," he'd say.

I knew it was a mistake to marry him but I was pregnant and I let him talk me into it.

"Don't you see?" he said. "This is just what I need to get myself together."

For a couple of weeks there I thought we had a real shot at being happy.

I didn't know some of his friends were doing harder stuff. I guess he did tell me about some guy he knew who had tried heroin. Once, he said. But Ben always swore he would never shoot up. For one thing, he was afraid of needles.

Well, I thought, that's good.

Then I guess he got one of his friends to do it for him, so he wouldn't fuck it up—his biggest fear.

When I found out, I let him know how disappointed I was.

He said, "I'm disappointed in myself."

I thought he was done, and that's what he led me to believe, but he kept doing it, I guess. He overdosed and actually died at one point, but the medics were able to revive him.

I felt bad about leaving him but I couldn't hang around after that.

He keeps telling me not to give up on him. He just got out of rehab, not for the first time. It's good he keeps trying.

WHATSHISNAME

I'm in the back part of the kitchen by the big double sink, skinning and gutting twenty pounds of calamari, when Spencer comes around the corner.

"That guy you saw Naomi with, what did he look like?"

"I don't know, tall?"

"Would you recognize him if you saw him again?"

I stop what I'm doing and wipe off my hands—they're starting to itch as they often do when I handle calamari.

"Maybe."

The chef calls out an order and Spencer calls back, "Be right there!"

We go to the pantry window, and Spencer points out a guy in the dining room.

"That him?"

I can only see a partial profile as the guy turns toward Naomi, who seems to be giving his table extra attention. She touches his shoulder in a very familiar way before walking away with maybe a little extra sway in her hips.

"Hey, I've got an idea," I say. "Let's ask Naomi."

I think Spencer would like to go out there right now, but he has to hustle back to the line. He throws two salmon fillets on the grill. Then he's back.

"You think he looks like her?" he asks.

"No, I think she's much prettier, don't you?"

"Ha-ha. Word is she called him Jason."

"So?"

"So I don't see any family resemblance, do you?"

"Again I say: So?"

"So Jason is NOT Naomi's brother."

"Right, because her brother's name is Peter."

"Jason. You said it was Jason."

Shit! I promised Naomi I wouldn't tell Spencer and now I've made the same slip she made with me.

"No," I say.

"Yes, you did. You both did."

"Look, there must be a million guys named Jason."

"So that's not the guy you met?"

"Her brother lives in Boston, doesn't he?"

"Right, so who is this guy?"

I don't answer but I don't even know who I'm trying to protect. Naomi? Spencer? Both?

SCORCHED

I'd really like a grilled cheese sandwich for lunch, but the frying pan is dirty. Scorched, actually.

"Looked at this," I say. "What do you suppose this was?"

"That? It was Hamburger Helper," Marty says. "I sort of forgot it was cooking."

"So ... Were you planning to wash this?"

"Yeah, I'll get to it."

"How about doing it now?"

"I'll do it later."

"But I'd really like to use it now."

"Then you wash it."

"Why should I clean up your mess?"

"Tell you what," he says, "you can leave it dirty when you're done and I'll clean it when I need it."

I'm too angry to speak. I start to clean the pan, or try to, but then I discover we're out of bread. Fuck it.

SOMETHING BLUE

Real weddings aren't like the ones you see on TV. The minister never asks if anyone has any objections.

That's probably not a surprise to you, but this is my first one.

"They stopped doing that a long time ago," Nita tells me, brushing stray strands of hair (black now, not pink or blue or fire-engine red) from the corner of her mouth. "Why? You want to stop the proceedings?"

I shake my head, eyes front. I can feel Nita looking at me, though. I'm pretty sure she's shaking her head, too. She may also be smiling; I can't be sure. (I tend to amuse her in ways I can't quite fathom.)

Anyway, I'm just here to bestow the honor of my presence on Tanya Alvarez and Trevor McKesson, as requested. The whole business strikes me as surreal, though. I keep wondering when, if ever, Tanya has been in a church before, and what, if anything, she has on under that long white gown.

Totally inappropriate, I know, but it wasn't all that long ago that I was fucking her on a regular basis. Now, here she is giving herself to this guy in a way she never gave herself to me.

YOU BLEW IT, BUSTER

Nita and I are in a motel on Highway One near Half Moon Bay. The room is dark. The window is open. We can hear ocean waves in the distance.

"You like that?"

"Mmmm..."

"You want me to do it some more?"

"Uh-huh."

"What are you going to do for me?"

A truck rumbles by on the highway, and in the silence that follows I realize my mistake.

"You don't have to do anything," I say. "Just enjoy it."

Waves crash. That's all.

Nita says, "You blew it, buster."

"You don't have to do anything. I like doing it."

"Well, that's what I thought."

"I just wanted to see if I could get you so turned on you'd do anything."

"I'll remember that."

"I just say whatever comes into my head. I never know if I'm going to say something wrong."

I hear her fumble with her purse and stuff on the nightstand, then see the flash of her lighter, the glow of her cigarette—the same kind Isla Fisher smokes in that movie with Ryan Reynolds.

"It's OK," she says.

"They say you shouldn't be held responsible for anything you say in the heat of passion."

"I know."

She puts out her cigarette.

MARTY MOVES OUT

Marty is moving out of the house in Sunnyvale.

That's the good news. (Much as I like the guy, he's a pain in the ass as a roommate.)

The bad news? My share of the rent just doubled.

Marty is moving in with the mysterious Fredson. No surprise there. But get this: Fredson is bankrolling Marty's new venture.

What new venture, you ask? A drive-up espresso stand—Espresso Ecstasy—in a parking lot on El Camino.

Marty scoped out the location, kept tabs on commuter traffic, talked to suppliers, and put together a business plan. The bank turned him down. Fredson did not.

I still have no idea what Fredson's first name is.

FORTUNE

"You will always get what you want through your charm and personality."

INTERVIEW

I take the fortune cookie as a good omen, because I have an actual job interview for an actual teaching job.

My feelings are decidedly mixed, though.

The opening is in a small town in the Central Valley. Farmland.

"You have to start somewhere," my dad tells me.

I know, I know ...

I drive out there and the countryside is beautiful, the town charming. It has one of everything: a school, a bank, a church, a restaurant, a doctor, a dentist.

The principal, Mrs. Hughes, is a middle-aged blonde who dresses like Hilary Clinton. I'm perfectly calm and the interview goes well.

I'm perfectly calm until I start the drive home.

Then I start shaking so bad I have to white-knuckle the steering wheel to steady myself. It's already August. School will be starting in a few weeks.

THE OTHER GUY

Naomi finally gives up.

"OK, OK," she says. "Jason is not my brother."

Spencer folds his arms and waits.

"But I wasn't cheating on you; I was cheating on him."

I'm sitting in the backyard—feet up, beer in hand—while Naomi and Spencer talk it out in the house. They know I'm right here on the other side of the screen door but make no effort to lower their voices. I look away, look up into the giant Japanese maple spreading its branches over the yard.

"Say what?"

"Jason and I have been together for two years, but he travels a lot and I get lonely."

"So I'm the other guy."

"Yes."

"And ... what the fuck, Naomi?"

"I know. I'm sorry. I can't choose. How am I supposed to choose?"

Suddenly all is quiet.

The silence continues so I finish my beer and go inside for another. I don't see Naomi and Spencer, but I can hear them in the bedroom.

Not their voices but the sounds they make.

Did not see that coming.

NITA TRIES HUMOR

Here's Nita's latest story:

Correction

I was pleased to learn that California has a Corrections Department, with an office in San Francisco. I gave them a call.

"Hello, Department of Corrections? I'd like to have a correction made on my driver's license. I've changed hair colors since this was issued ..."

"You'll need to call the Department of Motor Vehicles."

"Wait a minute, this is the Corrections Department, right?"

"Yes, but—"

"Well, this is a very simple correction. I used to have black hair, now ..."

"I'm sorry, this is where you call if you're on parole from prison. You need to call Motor Vehicles."

"You can't make this correction for me?"

"No."

"What do you correct?"

"I told you: this is the number to call if you're on parole."

"I see. Have you ever thought about changing your name?"

"No, have you ever thought about calling the Motor Vehicles Department so they can help you?"

The line went dead.

Oh, well, I'm sure the DMV will fix me up in a snap. You know, come to think of it, my address had changed, too.

—ANITA CHAN

The funniest part is that Nita's editor likes the story so much he decides to finally hire her and pay her and everything.

BIG MAN

Spencer and I are already on the court when Marty shows up, riding in the passenger seat of a new Q37 convertible. Jackie, who I haven't seen since the skirmish in the park, is behind the wheel. She kisses Marty before he gets out and watches as he walks toward us, admiring his swagger.

"You back with Jackie?"

She honks, waves, and drives away. Marty grins.

"Funny how a new car can turn a girl's head."

"That was YOUR car?"

"What can I say? Business is good."

I toss him the ball and he throws up a brick that hits the backboard but not the rim. From the look on his face, though, you'd think he just scored the winning basket in game seven.

Spencer shakes his head, sinks a twenty-footer.

"You must be turning out a hell of a lot of cappuccino," he says, "to buy a ride like that."

"Company vehicle," Marty says. "One of the perks of being your own boss."

"I thought Fredson was the boss."

"Nope, silent partner."

BLUE STATION WAGON

We arrive in Santa Cruz in my ancient silver Scirocco and breathe a sigh of relief to be off the highway at last. Then a woman in a small blue station wagon changes lanes and nearly sideswipes us. As we approach the next intersection, the light turns red.

"Oh, good," I say. "I'll be able to flip her off."

"I already looked at her."

"So did I."

We pull up beside her.

"She won't look now, she's too … Oh, look, there's a dent in her car. Wonder how that got there."

You probably don't find that terribly amusing. I do. I don't know why, really. Maybe it's just that it makes me feel close to Nita. Like we see things the same way. Like we could be some old married couple or something.

Is that what I want?

Maybe. I don't know. Probably.

EXPLAINS A LOT

My mother tried to abort me with a stick so my dad would never know she was pregnant again.

I know this because my mother later confided in one of my sisters, who confided in me.

I don't blame my mother. She was thirty-five and already had three kids.

I don't know why my sister decided to tell me about it. She wasn't being mean, if that's what you're thinking. I get along well with all three of my sisters. Always have.

They all doted on me when I was a tyke.

Which probably explains a lot. I don't know. You tell me: Am I spoiled? I think I probably am in some ways.

I'm like a puppy who wags his tail and expects everyone to love him and pet him. Except my earliest unconscious memory (the bottom of the iceberg, deep below the surface) is of someone trying to kill me.

THE OTHER HALF

By the time we find a place to park, we have to walk three blocks back to the house, then follow the curving driveway to the top of the hill. From there we can look down on 280 (the world's most beautiful highway, if you can believe the signs) and see the flow of white and red lights moving in opposite directions.

The house itself is much bigger than I would have imagined.

"This is where Marty lives?" Nita asks.

None of us can quite believe it.

Tiki lights illuminate the path to the backyard, and we follow along, all smiles, Nita and I in step behind Spencer and Naomi, who is wearing a little staples dress, white with big red polka dots, and red pumps.

"Do you ever think about Naomi when you masturbate?" Nita asks.

"What? No!"

"Hmm, I do."

She takes my arm and rests her cheek against my shoulder.

"If that's supposed to turn me on," I say, "it's working."

We enter the backyard through a Bougainvillea-covered archway. A band is playing Beck covers over waves of small talk and drunken giggles from a hundred guests we don't recognize.

A young woman in a black skirt and white blouse offers us champagne, and we all take plastic flutes from her silver tray.

"Welcome, my friends!"

It's Marty, who has suddenly appeared behind us with Jackie on his arm. She smiles and leans against him, her face flushed.

"So this is how the other half lives," Naomi says.

Spencer shakes Marty's hand and then so do I.

"I guess this beats sharing a bunk bed with me, eh?"

"Got that right," Marty says. "Come on, I'll give you the tour."

We catch a couple going at it on a king-size bed in the first bedroom. They keep going as if we're not there, but with maybe a little more intensity. Athletes responding to the crowd. We're only murmuring, though, not cheering. Not that they aren't phenomenal fuckers.

Naomi looks as if she'd like to join them. She nudges Spencer. He smiles but shakes his head.

Marty tries to show us the main bathroom, but the door is locked so we move to the kitchen, where caterers surround a massive marble-topped island. They're replenishing trays with prawns, crab cakes, caviar, brie, and bruschetta.

"Bring us a tray in the living room," Marty says.

An older blonde looks up and says, "Right away, sir."

The living room is dark and quiet (off limits to other guests) and has an expansive view of the darkening valley. Jackie excuses herself and rushes off in search of an unoccupied bathroom, her six-inch heals click-clacking against the tile floor. I think she's going to be sick.

"The couple who own this place are spending the summer in Tuscany," Marty says. "Fredson and I are just looking after it for them, but he really wants to buy the place. He's going to make an offer if his latest deal pans out."

"Speaking of Fredson," I say, "where is he?"

"Upstairs, talking to a couple of Sand Hill suits."

I ask about the deal, but Marty won't talk about it.

"Fredson is super secretive," he says. "He doesn't want anyone stealing his ideas."

We all nod, nibble hors d'oeuvres, and admire the view.

THE OTHER GUY, REVISITED

Spencer and I are shooting hoops in the park, and he is sinking everything. He's not even trying, just flipping the ball toward the basket and watching it drop through.

I'm lucky to hit one in three.

Pretty soon I just station myself under the net and feed him the ball. He sinks five in a row, six, seven. I'm dumbfounded; he's down in the dumps. I ask him why.

"Why do you think?"

"Naomi?"

Spencer nods. Eight in a row.

"What now?"

"What do you think?"

I take a wild guess.

"Jason?"

"Is there someone else?"

I shake my head, pass him the ball.

"Doesn't he live in Boston? What's he doing out here again so soon?"

"Her brother lives in Bean Town. This joker lives in Lala Land."

Nine in a row. He wasn't even looking.

"Tell her to make up her mind," I say.

"Yeah? What if she chooses him?"

"Then you move on."

"You don't get it. She's like a drug, man. I'm hooked. I need that next high."

"What about her mood swings?" I say. "You can hardly stand to be around her then."

Spencer finally misses; I chase down the ball.

"You know what?" he says. "That's a small price to pay."

I pass him the ball once more.

"Really? You didn't seem to think so at the time."

"I can hardly remember the last time she got like that."

He starts pacing, dribbling back and forth around the perimeter. After a minute, he looks at me.

"Think you could do it?"

"What?"

"Say no to Naomi."

I shrug.

"Don't kid yourself. You wouldn't last five minutes with her if she wanted you."

He drives in hard for a layup.

"Ha!" I say. "I bet I could go six."

THREE SURPRISES

Nita walks over to the jukebox and puts on a song by this band called Camera Obscura.

The thing about the Backstreet Bar & Grill is (in addition to stellar brews and killer sandwiches) it has this crazy-cool jukebox, with songs by Jack Johnson, Johnny Cash, B.B. King, Madonna, The Beatles, Bruno Mars, Alicia Keyes, Foster the People, Van Morrison, Taylor Swift, The Beach Boys, Bad Religion, and the aforementioned Camera Obscura.

The song Nita picks is really dreamy stuff, makes me feel like I did when my heart was new.

Then comes the first of three surprises:

Nita stops by the table where Ariel and a fellow cougar are having a couple of pints and scoping the place out (which has been distracting me all night). She then takes Ariel's face in her hands and kisses her full on the lips. She does this briefly, a little longer, and a lot longer.

The second surprise:

Just as we're all about to fall off our bar stools, Nita takes Ariel's hand and leads her toward the exit.

The third surprise:

Halfway to the door, Nita turns to me and says, "Are you coming or what?"

AFTER

I make it home sometime after noon.

"So," Spencer says, "you, Nita, and Ariel. Good times?"

He and Marty are sharing a joint in the living room.

I just smile.

Marty inhales and holds the smoke in his lungs as long as he can. Finally, he lets it out.

"What's this? Did I hear right?" he says. "You have a three-way or something?"

I flop down on the carpet, shake my head.

"You dog! You did! Don't lie to me. I can tell you did. Now, we want to hear ALL about it."

"No way."

"Come on, man. Spill it."

"I did. With Nita and Ariel."

"Ho-ho, that's the spirit. Details, man. We must have details."

"It's none of your business."

"Did you both do Ariel and then ..."

"I'm not telling you anything, Marty."

"I bet Nita sat on your face while Ariel rode …"

"Look, we are not talking about this."

Finally, Spencer interrupts: "Let it go, Marty."

"I need to know," he protests. "I need to know so I can be all worldly and shit when I get my chance."

"Yeah, right, that'll happen."

"It happened to Luke."

"You're right," Spencer says. "Could happen to anyone."

RAVENOUS

No, I'm not going to tell you about that night either. But I will share this:

We slept late and eventually gathered in Ariel's kitchen. I was the first one there and started making coffee. Then Nita came in and started cracking eggs into a bowl. Finally, Ariel got the bacon going.

No one said a word but we were all smiling.

The kitchen seemed small with everyone in it. We slid past each other silently, sleepily, rubbing up against one another "accidentally," Nita in her T-shirt, Ariel in a silk chemise, me in my boxers.

We all made ourselves busy setting the small round table in the breakfast nook, but never too busy to squeeze a bending booty or fondle a passing pair of ta-tas. There was a lot of kissing, too. If I kissed Nita, I needed to kiss Ariel as well, who then had to kiss Nita.

At some point, Nita and Ariel decided my boxers no longer looked comfortable, so they removed them for me.

"That's better," they said in unison.
Then we ate.

BACKSTORY

Ariel married young and had a daughter, Nadia, who died when she was sixteen, texting while driving.

They had given Nadia the smart phone for her birthday, so she could always call home if she had car trouble or drank too much at a party or some jerk was hassling her or whatever.

She knew better than to use it while driving, and yet …

That's as much as I have ever gotten from Ariel. She doesn't like to talk about it, which I totally understand, but I have always felt like she doesn't talk about it at least in part because I so clearly don't know what to say.

Ariel once told Nita, who later told me, that she would never have another child, which drove a wedge between her and her husband, who did not believe her when she said she was too old now.

Ariel did want sex, though, and lots of it, the kinkier the better. That kept her husband happy, for a while.

We all do our best not to think about it.

TICKLE COASTER

Kayla has discovered tickling. She especially enjoys being tickled.

Now, whenever I stop by, she waits for me to sit down, then climbs into my lap, and says, "Tickle me."

Sometimes I pretend not to hear and go on talking to Nita, but before long my fingers find their way into Kayla's ribs and peels of laughter fill the air.

She squirms away but soon comes back.

After she falls off my lap this time I insist that she fasten her seatbelt, which consists of my arm draped across her torso, my right hand snapping into my left with a reassuring snick from my teeth and tongue.

"Now," I ask her, "are you ready to ride the Tickle Coaster?"

She is. Again and again.

THE FOURTH CONVERTIBLE

It's a hot day and we're sitting at a table on the sidewalk sipping lemonade and waiting for our burgers to arrive.

Nita says, "That's the fourth convertible I've seen go by."

"So why should that bother you?"

"It shouldn't," she says. "And it doesn't."

"I didn't think it would."

"Bastards."

DADDY ISSUES

Sunday afternoon. Chan residence.

We're sitting on the front porch and I'm sharing an Almond Joy with Kayla despite Nita's (feigned) disapproval.

I know, I know, I'm spoiling her, but you should see the look on her face: Pure delight. No artificial additives. Nothing held back.

God, it's beautiful.

Then I see this guy striding across the lawn.

"You're not her father," he says.

"No, I'm Luke."

"Well, I'm Kayla's dad."

"Pleased to meet you."

He doesn't shake my hand or tell me his name. Nita has to do that.

"This is Ben," she says. "Ben, are you high?"

Ben ignores her.

"You think you can step into my shoes, is that it?"

"Uh, no."

Nita tries to tell him to relax, but he continues to ignore her.

"Kayla has a daddy," he says. "Me."

"We're just, uh, sharing a candy bar."

"A little candy bar. See, Daddy? Just the right size for me."

Kayla shows him the remaining half of her half of the Almond Joy. Ben gives her a quick (feigned) smile and turns back to me.

"I need to talk to my family," he says. "Why don't you get lost?"

"Ben! Don't be a—"

"It's OK," I say. "I was just leaving."

"You know," Nita says, "I can have your visiting rights revoked."

Ben shuts up and sits down. Kayla is crying quietly. I wish I could do something.

FANTASTIC

I strip off my sweats, wrap a towel around my waist, and head down the hall to the bathroom. Just as I arrive the door opens.

It's Naomi. Naked.

Her hair is wet and drops of water roll down her shoulders. I want to follow them down farther, but I don't.

Our eyes lock.

She smiles, I think, and pretty soon I smile.

We stand like that, eye to eye and toe to toe, for about three hours. Then she reaches for a towel and covers herself.

It takes me a while to realize the towel she has taken is mine, so now I'm the one who is naked. She is definitely smiling now, but she is no longer looking into my eyes.

We're all of about twelve inches apart and without moving I am able to cover about half that distance.

Naomi waits and watches.

"You can do it," she says. "Just a little farther."

We're an inch closer.

"Here," she says. "Maybe this will help."

She drops the towel.

Oh, my god, I grow two more inches. Three, I swear. We're almost touching now. Millimeters apart.

"Close enough," she says and leaps into my arms, her legs wrapping around my hips.

Spencer comes out of his room with a stopwatch.

"Go!" he says.

TO ME

Even in my fantasies things happen TO me. The difference is they happen just the way I want them to.

INTENTIONS

Nita's mom wants to know my intentions.

"We're going to a club to hear some music, dance …"

Mrs. Chan, tiny but imposing, folds her arms.

"That's not what I mean," she says.

I know what she means and she knows I know, but still I stall for time.

"Oh," I say. "What do you mean?"

She tilts her head and stares at me. I feel as if I'm waiting for my prom date. What the hell is taking Nita so long?

"I'm very fond of your daughter," I say.

"And Kayla?"

Kayla is putting a puzzle together on the kitchen table.

"Her, too," I say.

Mrs. Chan shakes her head.

"You better think about what you're getting into," she says.

"I know."

"Do you? I don't think so."

Then it hits me. She's right. I don't know.

OVERDOSE

I'm already at work when my mobile vibrates in my pocket.

"Dude, you have to get over here."

"Why? What happened? What's wrong?"

"Just, dude, please."

"What is it? What happened, Marty?"

"It's Fredson. I think he ..."

"What?"

"OD'ed. I think he OD'ed, man."

"Call nine-one-one."

"I can't."

"You have to."

"What if he wakes up and the police start asking questions? He'll kill me."

"Easy, big guy, we're talking about paramedics here, not police officers. Check his pulse. Does he have a pulse?"

"I don't know. Maybe. I feel a heartbeat but I think it's mine."

"Is he breathing?"

"This is bad. This is so bad."

"Marty, listen, hold a mirror up to his nose, see if he fogs the mirror."

"What do you think, Luke? You think I'm going to reach into my purse and pull out a mirror? The only mirror here is on the bathroom wall. Maybe I should just hold him up to the medicine cabinet."

"You have to call nine-one-one."

"He'll kill me. The paramedics will tell the police and Fredson will kill me."

"He's not going to kill you. The police will be there."

"Not right away. Later."

"They'll take him to jail, Marty."

"He'll get out. His lawyers will get him out. Or he'll have one of his henchmen kill me."

"He has henchmen?"

"I don't know. Probably."

FUNERAL FOR A FRIEND

Fredson's body lies in a closed casket in a small church in San Jose. It's a drab place. Nothing ornate about it.

The minister introduces us to Fredson's parents, Harvey and Bev.

Marty covers his surprise with a show of delight.

"Pleased to finally meet you," he says.

All this time he has assumed Fredson was living (and partying) off a trust fund left to him by wealthy parents, but these folks are shy and shabby looking.

"Freddy was such a fine boy," his mother says. "I don't know what we're going to do without him."

Marty says he feels the same way. He means it, too.

If I'm not mistaken there was a tear in Marty's eye when he returned the Q37 to the dealer. Fortunately, his name was not on the lease.

Of course he knew Fredson dabbled in the drug trade (as did he), but he thought it was just a rich boy's thrill-seeker hobby.

Aside from Fredson's parents and the balding, brown-suited minister, Marty and I are the only ones at the funeral.

DOWNHEARTED

Here's the problem: I've never really wanted children.

It's not that I don't like them. My sisters all have kids and they're adorable. Until they're not.

Until they cry and shit themselves.

Until they scream and throw things.

Until they refuse to go to bed or get dressed or eat their vegetables.

Don't get me wrong. I love them all. I do. I just don't want to be around them when they're being obstinate. You can't reason with them and, all kidding aside, you can't really punch them. We've established that, right?

So what am I getting myself into? How involved do I really want to be with Nita and her little one?

I mean, it's great right now. It's wonderful, in fact. But what happens when it's not?

SUSPECT ARRESTED

Now investigators are asking questions Marty can't answer and finding things he can't explain. Like a ledger tracking the sale of stocks, bonds, mutual funds, and derivatives to investors who are identified only by their initials.

It doesn't take them long to surmise that the financial instruments are code words for drugs of various kinds.

Marty is shocked. If that's true, he swears, he had no clue.

Fredson kept the books for Espresso Ecstasy as well.

"Math was never my strong suit," Marty says.

As it turns out, the police can find no evidence linking Marty to the heroine trade, but they do arrest one of Fredson's buyers: Ben Stafford, Nita's former husband.

His arrest is almost immediate: His fingerprints are all over the place, and this is not his first run-in with the police.

They charge him with robbery, possession, and intent to sell.

They might have added murder—Ben had motive, means, and opportunity—except there was no evidence of a struggle.

HELLO, STRANGER

I run into Nita at the grocery. She has Kayla with her, riding in her shopping cart.

"Hello, stranger," she says. "Where have you been keeping yourself?"

I don't have a good answer.

Kayla is smiling and holding out her arms. I pretend not to notice.

"So," I say, "how about you? Run out of Cheerios?"

She looks at me for a long time, then wheels her cart around and heads down the aisle.

It hurts like hell, but I let them go.

FAREWELL, NAOMI

The next thing I know Spencer and Naomi are no more.

It takes me a while to catch on, but pretty soon I detect a pattern: She doesn't come in to work, she doesn't come by the house ...

"What gives?" I ask.

"She's gone," he says. "Gone to L.A."

"For what?"

"Forever, I guess."

"No way."

We're at Bistro 227, after hours, having a couple of beers at the U-shaped bar.

"I told her to choose," he says, "and she did."

"Fuck!"

"Not anymore."

He sort of laughs, but there's no mirth.

"She chose him? That's insane."

We finish our beers and order more.

LAID BARE

Two days later, I get home and, almost as soon as I close the door, someone knocks.

It's Nita.

"I am so—"

She reaches out and presses her finger to my lips so I can say no more. Then she takes my hand and leads me down the hall and into the room I am once again sharing with Marty.

She closes the door and locks it.

Again I start to speak; again she silences me.

The next thing I know we're on the floor. She kisses me and peels off my shirt. She kisses me and peels off my pants, shoes, socks, everything. She pins me down and kisses me some more. Then she slides up and straddles my face. She's not wearing anything under her skirt.

She comes and fucks me and comes again.

Finally she wears herself out and we fall asleep on the floor. When I awake, she's gone. The house is dark and I can hear Marty snoring on the sofa.

GONE

I go looking for Nita the next day, but she's nowhere to be found.

I keep looking all week but see no sign of her or Kayla or even her battered old Volvo. She doesn't answer my calls, texts, or emails.

I knock on her door and ask her mother: "Is Nita home?"

Mrs. Chan shakes her head.

"Do you know where she is?"

She pretends not to understand, but there's something in her face that reminds me of the ferocity her daughter showed when she laid me bare and fucked my brains out.

Mrs. Chan says something in Chinese and closes the door.

THAT NIGHT

I can't stop thinking about that night—the last night we spent together.
 The locked door.
 Nita's insistence on silence.
 Then the shattering noises she made.
 The anger I mistook for passion.

BY ACCIDENT

Quite by accident I run into Ariel on Santana Row. She seems offended somehow even before I say hello.

I still have fond memories of our three-way but it was never repeated, by silent consensus. In any case, none of us ever spoke of it. So why the cold shoulder?

"Have you seen Nita?" I ask.

She would like to go around me but the sidewalk is crowded with trendy shoppers, so she simply stares at me stone faced.

Suddenly I know where Nita is. Ariel confirms it.

"Don't you dare come around my door," she says.

OFFICE VISIT

I find the address of the magazine and drive up to the city. I don't want to do this, but it seems like my only chance.

The receptionist asks if she can help me.

"Um, yeah, I'd like to speak to Nita Chan."

She picks up the phone.

"Is she expecting you?"

"No, I'm a ... a friend."

I smile and the receptionist smiles back.

"Your name?"

I say the first name that comes to mind. She punches in three numbers and waits.

"Nita? Tom Cruz is here to see you."

She hangs up the phone and smiles at me some more.

"She'll be right out, Mr. Cruz."

A minute later, Nita sees me and spins around. I follow her down the corridor.

"Wait!" I say.

"Go home," she says, still walking.

"Look, just let me—"

She stops, turns.

"Let you what? Let you explain?" she says. "You think I don't know? You think I don't get it? You think this hasn't happened to me more times than I care to count?"

I honestly, stupidly, did not think of that. I say nothing.

She shakes her head and tells me again to go home.

HOW IT FEELS

It's already dark by the time Nita emerges from her South-of-Market office building, her pleated skirt bouncing against her black tights, her high heels clicking on the sidewalk. I'm sitting across the street, having a drink. I run to catch up with her.

She won't stop so I walk alongside her.

"I told you to go home," she says.

"I miss you."

"Get over it."

We're in a parking garage now and she's unlocking her car, tossing her shoulder bag inside. I have to say something, but what?

"You fucked me."

This makes her smile, but not in a particularly good way. Her smile seems to recall satisfaction of more than one kind.

"You fucked me," I say, "and then you just ... ran."

Nita gets in her car.

"Now you know how it feels," she says.

A moment later the scent of burning rubber fills my nostrils.

LIFE, LIBERTY, AND THE PURSUIT

I'm driving around, listening to the radio, reading the road signs, billboards, and bumper stickers:

Bed, Bath & Beyond Now Open. Freeway Entrance. "Three-car collision, Willow at Bayfront." Lane Ends, Merge Left. Office Space Available. Mystery Spot. Under New Management. No Parking Anytime. Eyewitness News at 11. This Bitch Hauls Ass. Right Lane Must Exit.

I don't know where I'm going. I don't know what to do.

That school in the Central Valley? They want me to teach English to tenth-graders.

WELL AND TRULY

Nita has fucked me well and truly because I can't stop thinking about her.
    I want her to fuck me again.
    I want her to fuck me for the rest of my life.

TIME PASSES

I turn down the teaching job, which surprises me as much as it does Principal Hughes.

Then a month goes by in which I never see or hear from Nita.

I have driven out to Ariel's place in Los Altos several times, and I have seen Nita's car parked in the driveway, but I have resisted the urge to knock on the door.

I don't want to fight with both of them, especially not in front of Kayla, who I miss way more than I ever thought I would.

Time has passed but my feelings haven't. If I could just win them back, then I know we'd be happy.

But I guess they're happy without me.

FINALLY

When I can't stand it any longer, I walk down the street and knock on Mrs. Chan's door.

I have to knock again and again before she opens up.

"You were right," I tell her. "I didn't know what I was getting into."

She folds her arms.

"I know what I want now," I say. "I know beyond a shadow of a doubt. You have to help me."

She does not respond, which means this is going about as badly as I imagined it would. Still, I have to try.

"Please," I say. "I can't be happy without them."

Mrs. Chan looks over her shoulder, steps back, and swings the door open. There in the narrow hallway are Nita and Kayla.

We look at each other as the sun goes down and comes up again. No one says a word. The only sound comes from inside my ribcage, a drumbeat that vibrates the fabric of my shirt. I'm waiting for a sign but nobody moves.

    Finally I realize it's up to me and I step forward.

Also by Al Riske

Precarious
Sabrina's Window
The Possibility of Snow

About the author

Al Riske is a former newspaper reporter and magazine editor. Born and raised in the Pacific Northwest, he now lives in California with his wife, Joanne, and their dog, Bodie.

Made in the USA
Middletown, DE
31 January 2021